Inside All

by Margaret H. Mason

illustrated by Holly Welch

Dawn Publications

For my mother Shirley and my sister Dorothy
inside all of our hearts – MHM

For my boys: Shawno; Mason; and baby Summit,
who inspired me from the inside – HW

Copyright © 2008 Margaret H. Mason
Illustration copyright © 2008 Holly Welch

A Sharing Nature With Children Book

Library of Congress Cataloging-in-Publication Data
Mason, Margaret H., 1954-
 Inside all / by Margaret H. Mason ; illustrated by Holly Welch. -- 1st ed.
   p. cm. -- (A sharing nature with children book)
 Summary: Takes the reader on a nesting doll-like journey, from the edges
of the universe into the heart of a child at bedtime, showing how we each
have our place inside the universe and the universe has a place inside each
of us.
 ISBN 978-1-58469-111-2 (hardcover) -- ISBN 978-1-58469-112-9 (pbk.)
 [1. Stories in rhyme. 2. Universe--Fiction. 3. Bedtime--Fiction.] I.
Welch, Holly, ill. II. Title.
 PZ8.3.M41963In 2008
 [E]--dc22
                                      2008012260

Printed in China
10 9 8 7 6 5 4 3 2 1

First Edition

Design and computer production by Holly Welch
Computer production by Patty Arnold, Menagerie Design and Publishing

Dawn Publications
12402 Bitney Springs Road
Nevada City, CA 95959
530-274-7775
nature@dawnpub.com

A human being
is part of the whole,
called by us
the 'Universe' ...

— Albert Einstein

Inside all
Is a universe

Energy flowing.

Inside the universe
Is a galaxy

Milky and glowing.

Inside the galaxy
Is a planet

Blue and hopeful.

On the planet
Is a land

Green and growing.

Inside the land
Is a valley

Night winds blowing.

Inside the valley
Is a village

Twinkling lights showing

Inside the village
Is a home

Warm laughter floating,

Inside the home
Is a space

Hushed and golden.

Inside the space
Is a bed

Cuddled and cozy.

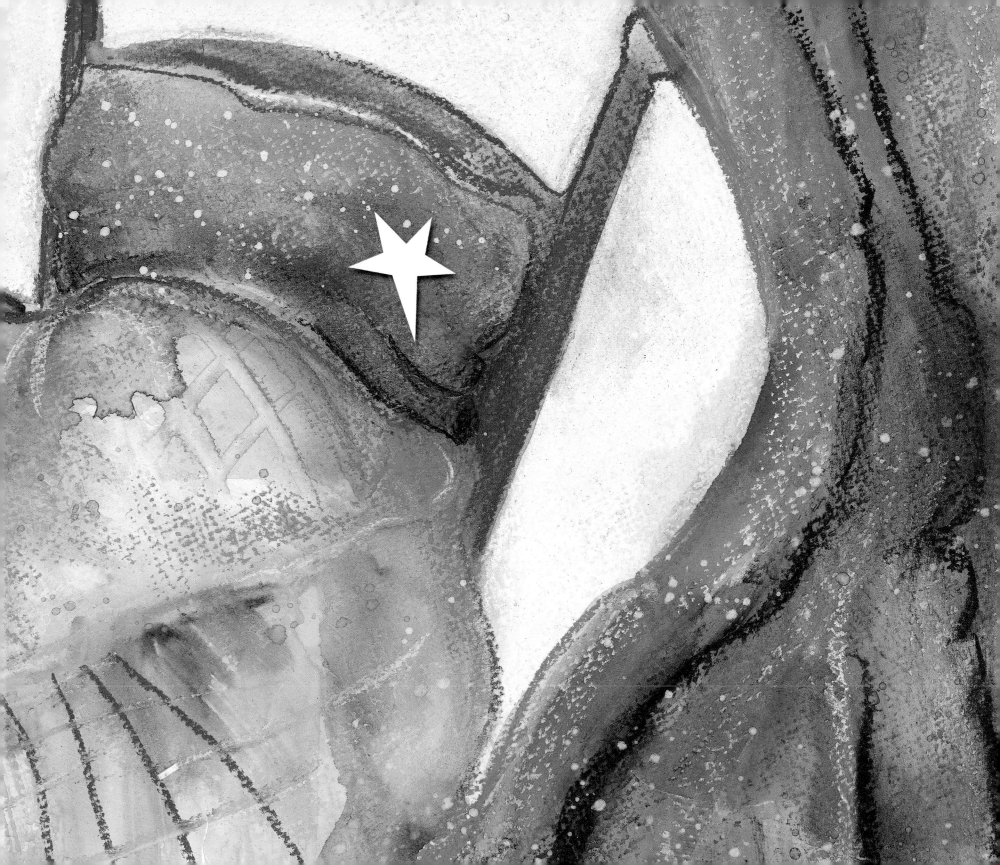

On the bed
Are covers

Deep and enfolding.

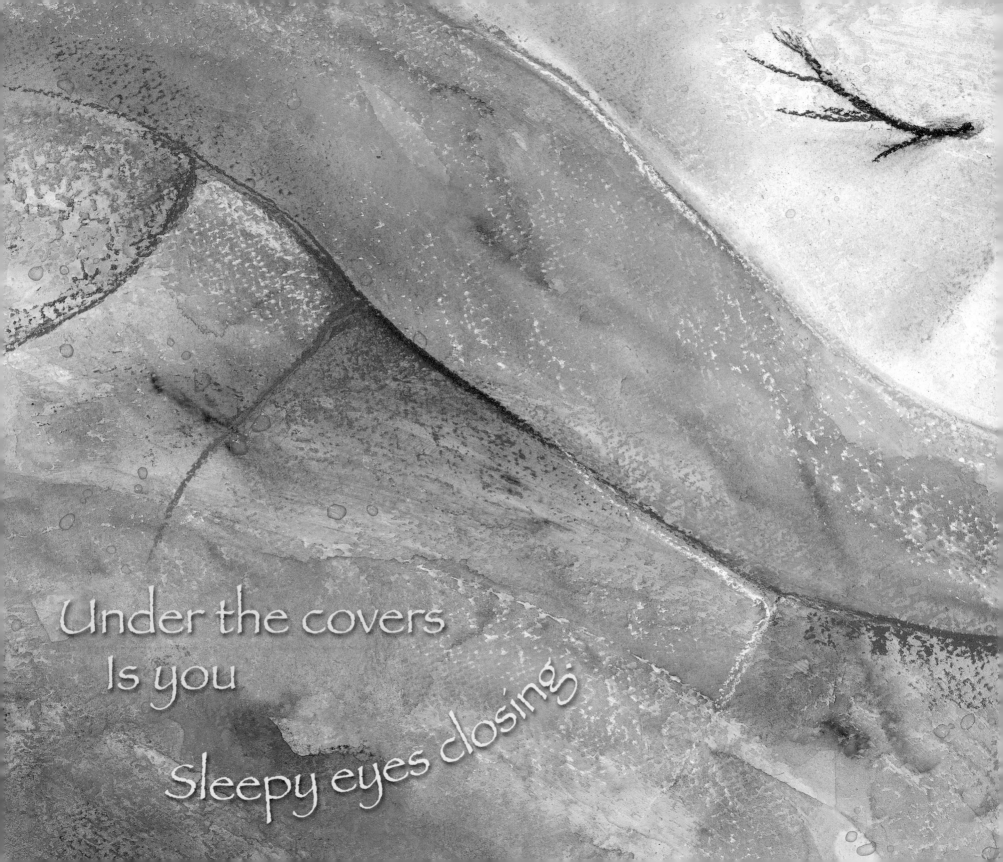

Under the covers
Is you

Sleepy eyes closing

Inside you
Is a heart

Pure and glowing.

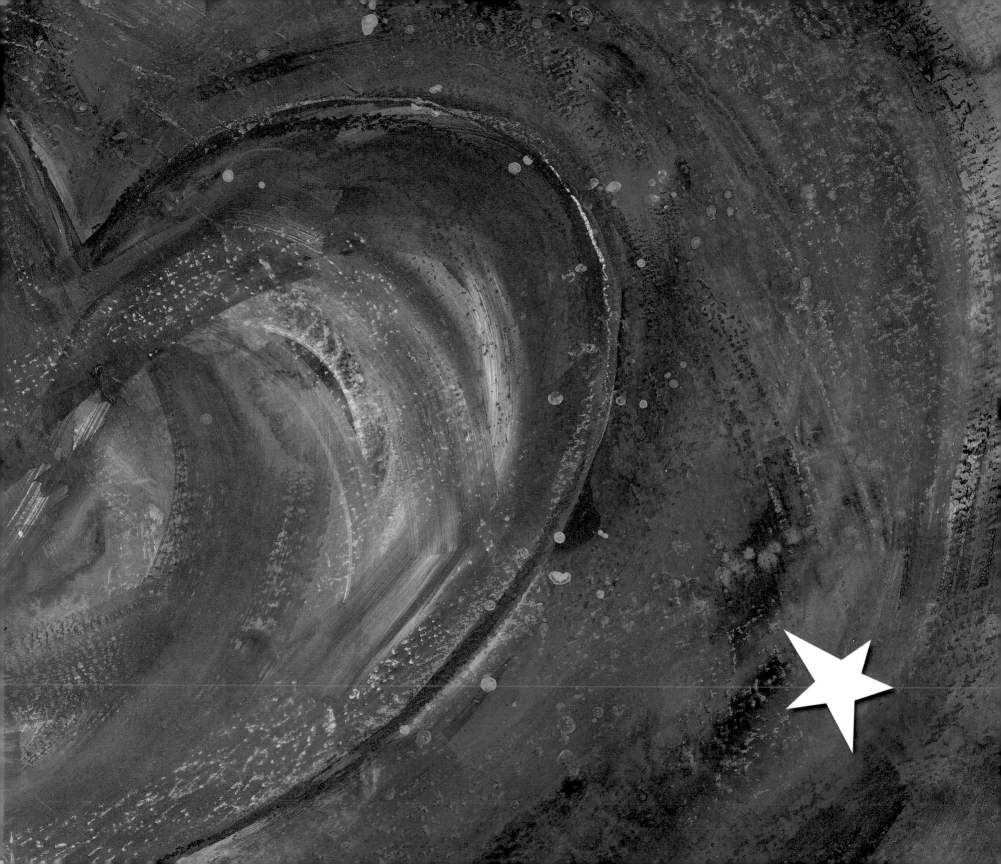

Inside your heart
Is all

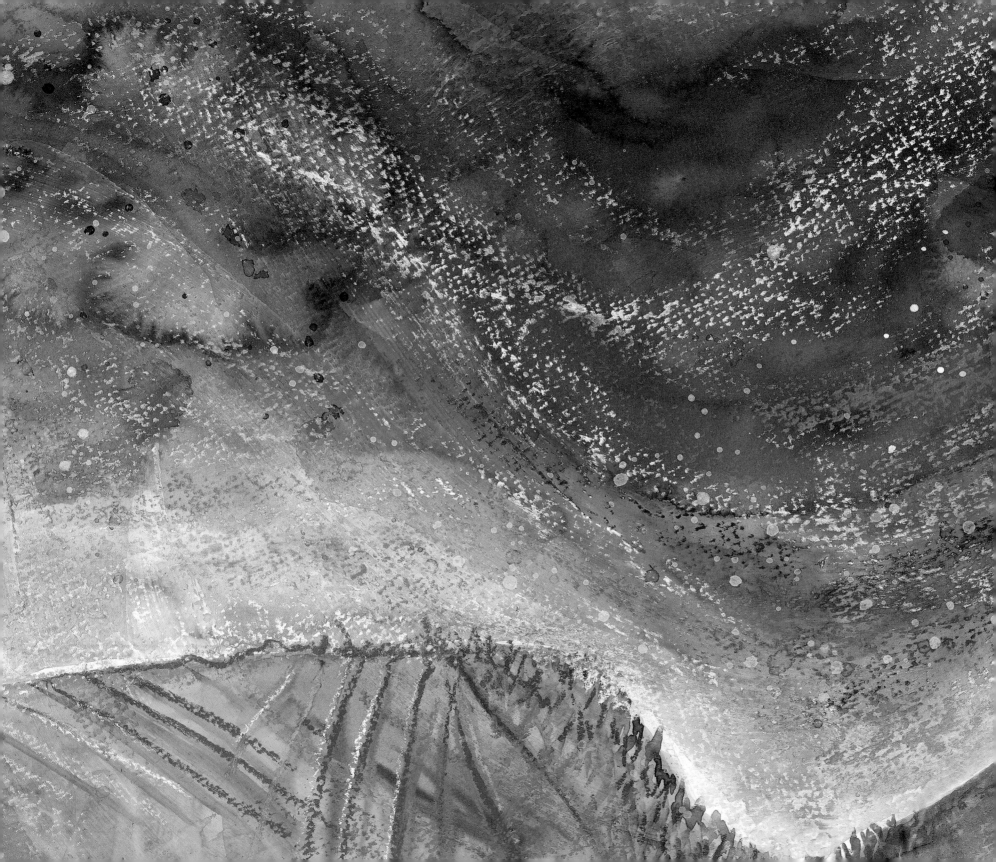

Looking at the sky one night, **Margaret H. Mason** had a vision. Starting with the great starry universe, it took her inside, and inside again, and finally into the heart of a child in bed—where she found the same great expanse as was in the beginning. With that vision came a great sense of security: that each of us belongs to the whole, and has a special place in it. Mason has a strong sense of the importance of belonging, a connection with nature, and a commitment to sharing both with children. She lives in Ferndale, Michigan and can also be found at www.callingmrtoad.com.

Holly Welch is an artist and graphic designer from Minneapolis, Minnesota, who loves color. Out of the blue, she got a job as a backpacking guide at a summer camp in Montana. She had hardly ever seen a mountain before. The experience changed her from a girl with a closet full of black clothes, yearning to live in Manhattan, to someone with hiking boots and a renewed dedication to creativity. Her sense of the earth, community and spirituality was shaped by the sound of the river, the chill of the mornings, and fields of wild daisies. She gave birth to her son Summit while working on this book— and feels that his presence on the inside influenced the images. Find her at www.hollywelchdesign.com.

A Few Other Nature Awareness Books from Dawn Publications

If You Were My Baby: A Wildlife Lullaby by Fran Hodgkins, illustrated by Laura J. Bryant, is a "sweet dream bedtime" book for nature lovers of all generations!

Eliza and the Dragonfly by Susie Rinehart, illustrated by Anisa Claire Hovemann, is a charming story revolving around the beauty and wonder of the hidden world that can be found in a local pond.

Forest Bright, Forest Night by Jennifer Ward, illustrated by Jamichael Henterly.
Take a peek into the forest in the daytime, then flip the book to see the same forest at nighttime.
Count the animals, and see who is asleep and who is busy!

All Around Me, I See by Laya Steinberg, illustrated by Cris Arbo.
With eyes wide open to the wonders of nature, a child, tired from her hike,
sleeps—and in her dream, flies like a bird and marvels at the life around her.

The John Denver & Kids Series: illustrator Christopher Canyon adapts some of John Denver's most delightful and uplifting lyrics: *Sunshine On My Shoulders, Take Me Home Country Roads, Grandma's Feather Bed* and *Ancient Rhymes: A Dolphin Lullaby.*

Dawn Publications is dedicated to inspiring in children a deeper understanding and appreciation for all life on Earth. To view our titles or to order, please visit us at www.dawnpub.com, or call 800-545-7475.